S0-BAI-451

Favorite Fairy Tales

TOLD IN GREECE

Favorite Fairy Tales

TOLD IN GREECE

Retold by Virginia Haviland

Illustrated by Martha Ploetz

FRANKLIN PIERCE
COLLEGE LIBRARY
RINDGE, N.H. 03461

A Beech Tree Paperback Book *New York*

Text copyright © 1970 by Virginia Haviland.
Illustrations copyright © 1996 by Martha Ploetz Walker.
All rights reserved. No part of this book may be reproduced or utilized in any form or by any means, electronic or mechanical, including photocopying, recording, or by any information storage and retrieval system, without permission in writing from the Publisher. Inquiries about the text should be addressed to Little, Brown and Co., 1271 Avenue of the Americas, New York, NY 10020. Inquiries about the art should be addressed to Beech Tree Books, William Morrow & Company, Inc., 1350 Avenue of the Americas, New York, NY 10019.

First Beech Tree Edition, 1996, published by arrangement with Little, Brown and Co.
Printed in the United States of America

10 9 8 7 6 5 4 3 2 1

These stories have been retold from the following sources:

"Constantes and the Dragon" and "The Foolish Wife and Her Three Foolish Daughters" are retold from E.M. Geldart's *Folklore of Modern Greece: The Tales of the People*. London, S. Swan Sonnenschein and Company, 1884.

"The Princess Who Loved Her Father Like Salt" is slightly adapted with the permission of The Clarendon Press, Oxford, from Richard McGillivray Dawkins's *Modern Greek Folktales*, 1953.

"The Fairy Wife," "The Wonder of Skoupa," "Fairy Gardens," "The First of May," and "Fairy Mother" are retold from *Fairy Tales of Modern Greece*, by Theodore P. Gianakoulis & Georgia H. MacPherson. Dutton, 1930.

Library of Congress Cataloging-in-Publication Data

Haviland, Virginia, 1911–
     Favorite fairy tales told in Greece / retold by Virginia Haviland ; illustrated by Martha Ploetz.
        p.   cm.
     Contents: Constantes and the dragon — The princess who loved her father like salt — The foolish wife and her three foolish daughters — The fairy wife — The wonder of Skoupa — Fairy gardens — The first of May — Fairy mother.
        ISBN 0-688-12597-2 (pbk.)
        1. Fairy tales — Greece.   [1. Fairy tales.   2. Folklore — Greece.]
     I. Ploetz, Martha, ill.   II. Title
     PZ8.H295Favd 1996
[398.2'09495]—dc20   94-35511
                                              CIP
                                              AC

CURR
PZ
8
.H295
Fvg
1996

Minor editorial and style changes have been made in the stories for these new editions.

Contents

Author's Note

IN GREEK FOLK STORIES, dragons and fairies are frequent characters. Both Dawkins's *Modern Greek Folktales* and Gianakoulis's *Fairy Tales of Modern Greece* have stories about the fairy wife, and in their respective tales, "The Mountain of Jewels and the Dove-Maiden" and "The Fairy Wife," there are similarities regarding the winning of the wife.

In the foreword to his *Fairy Tales of Modern Greece*, Gianakoulis accounts for nymphs as a surviving fragment of ancient Greek mythology: "For among the hills and across the fields and streams of Greece, where the gods were born and dwelt, fairies now dance and play and radiate a subtle charm. Fairies are none other than the modern forms of the dryads, oreads, naiads, nereids, fates, furies, graces, and muses of the ancient myths. They are the nymphs that sang and played with Pan and Hermes, Apollo and the satyrs, but now they play and dance and sing with common shepherds, fishermen, and hunters....

"Fashions in Greek fairy tales differ as much from

section to section as do customs and dialects. There are, however, certain universal fairy characteristics of which every Greek has heard and which are never disputed. There are the supernatural beauty of fairies, their love of the beautiful which makes them seek to carry away beautiful youths and maidens, their power over mortals, and their transition to a human, power-less state when an article belonging to them is in the possession of a mortal."

Constantes
and the Dragon

ONCE UPON A TIME there was an old man who had three sons, all three of whom were determined to go and learn a trade. So they set forth one day into the uplands in search of work.

When they discovered a field which had not been reaped, they said to each other, "Come, brothers, let us go in and cut the grain. Whoever owns it will pay us for our labor."

They set to work, but while they were reaping the mountains began to tremble, and they saw coming toward them a full-sized dragon. Believing the dragon to be the owner of the field, they tried to work even harder.

The dragon came close and said, "Good morrow, my lads."

"Good morrow, master," they answered.

"What are you doing here?" asked the dragon.

"We found this field unharvested and came in to cut the grain, for we knew that whoever owns it would pay us for our good labor."

They continued to work, and when they had cut half the grain, the dragon said to the youngest brother, who was called Constantes, "Do you see yonder mountain? There lives my wife. I want you to take this letter to her."

Constantes took the letter. Although he was the youngest, he was a cunning lad, and he decided that he would do well to read the letter before handing it to the dragon's wife. On the way he opened it, luckily, and in it he found these words: "The man I send you is to be killed at once. You must put him in the oven to cook, for I want him ready for my dinner when I come home tonight."

Constantes at once tore up the letter and wrote another one: "My dear dragoness — When the young man arrives with this letter, I beg you to kill our largest turkey for him. And you must fill a basket with bread loaves, and send him back with this food for the laborers."

Now when the dragon saw Constantes returning with a donkey heavily laden, he said to himself, "Ah, that fellow is a cleverer rogue than I!"

And to Constantes and his brothers he called out, "Come, friends, let us get through with this field quickly, and go to supper at my house so that I may pay you!"

Quickly they finished the reaping, whereupon

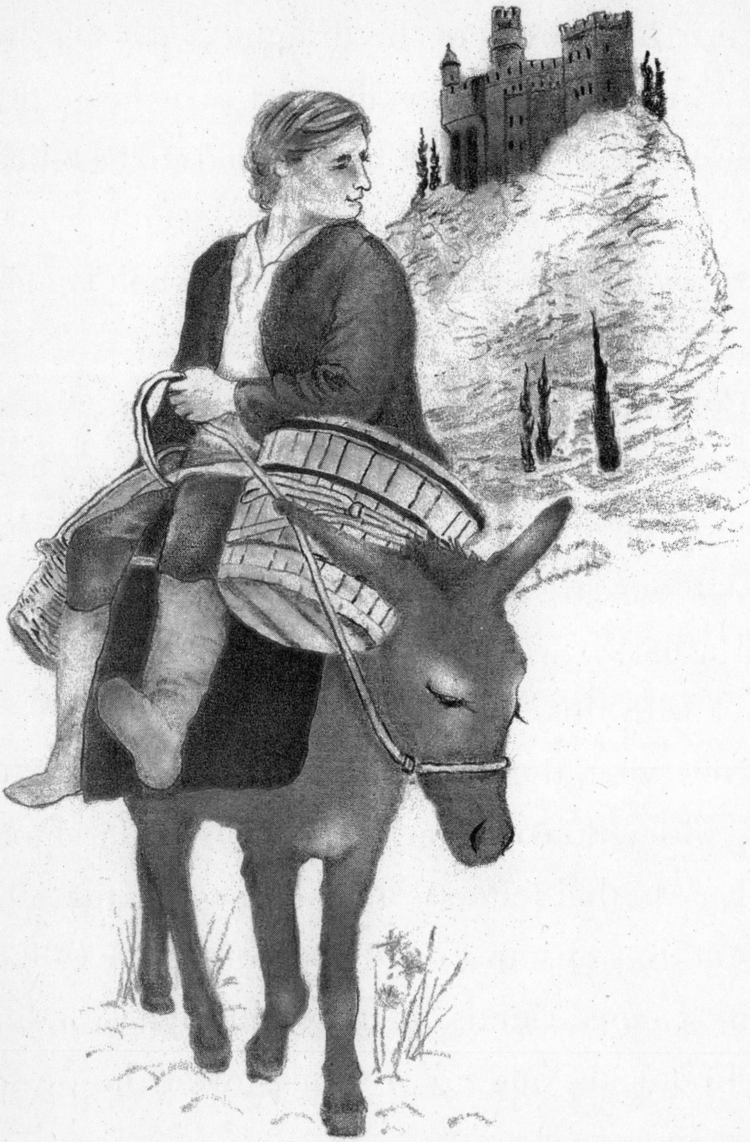

the dragon led them away. Secretly Constantes said to his brothers, "You have four eyes among you, brothers; you must keep wide awake to note where we are going."

That night after dinner, when the dragon and his wife had fallen asleep, Constantes got up and woke his brothers. Then he crept over to the dragoness and took her ring from her finger, very gently so that she did not feel it. The brothers ran off and had nearly reached the town when the dragon woke up and looked for them—now he was hungry and ready to eat them all. At that same moment the dragoness cried out that her ring was missing.

The dragon saw what had happened and sprang to his horse to go in search of the brothers. He spied them just as they were entering the town, and he called out, "Constantes, stop and let me pay you!"

But the brothers replied that they did not

want the pay, and they went on into town, ignoring the dragon's demand that they come back.

In the town they searched for work, and in a short time they were all in business—the eldest as a draper, the second as a carpenter, and Constantes as a tailor.

After a time the eldest brother became envious of Constantes because he had the ring. The brother decided on a plan to get rid of Constantes.

He went to the King and said, "Please, Your Majesty, you have many riches in your palace, but if you owned the dragon's diamond coverlet, you would stand alone among the monarchs of the earth."

"But how am I to get it?" asked the King. "Who is clever enough to fetch it for me?"

The brother then answered, "Let Your Majesty issue a proclamation saying that whoever shall fetch the dragon's coverlet will be made a great and mighty man. You must then summon my youngest brother, who is a tailor, and order him to get it for you. If he refuses, you will threaten to destroy him."

Accordingly the King issued a proclamation. But no one was brave enough to offer to go and fetch the coverlet. So the King had his vizier summon Constantes. He told Constantes that he must go to the dragon's home and steal the diamond coverlet. Constantes would be destroyed if he refused.

What could poor Constantes do? He had no choice but to set out on this mission. As he walked along, he prayed, "May the blessing of my mother and my father stand me in good stead now!"

He journeyed on and soon met an old woman to whom he bade his usual, "Good morrow."

"The same to you, my son!" said she. "And where are you going? You must know that whoever goes this way never lives to come back."

"The King has sent me to fetch him the dragon's diamond coverlet."

"Alas, my son, you will be lost!"

"But what can I do?"

"You must go back and tell those who sent you to give you three hollow reeds filled with insects. Then you must return to the dragon's house at night, when he is asleep. You will empty the reeds upon his coverlet. The dragon and his wife will not be able to endure the insects, so they will fling the coverlet over the window ledge and leave it hanging there. Then you must seize it and carry it off as fast as you can, for if the dragon catches you, he will eat you for sure."

The lad did exactly as the old woman told him, and he managed to run off with the coverlet.

When the dragon got up and discovered the coverlet missing, he called to his wife, "Where have you put the coverlet?"

"It's gone!" she cried.

"Ah, wife," said the dragon, "there is no one who can have taken it but Constantes." With that he again rushed to his stable, mounted his fastest horse, and in a short time caught up with Constantes.

"Give me that coverlet!" he demanded. "What trick have you been playing this time, you dog?"

But Constantes only replied, "What I have done thus far is nothing. Just wait for what I shall do to you next."

The dragon could not touch Constantes, for he was now entering the King's territory. Constantes was able to carry the coverlet to the King. The King's reward was an order for two suits of clothes.

After twenty days had passed, the jealous eldest brother went again to the King and said, "Please, Your Majesty, has Constantes brought you the dragon's diamond coverlet?"

The King answered, "Yes indeed, and a very fine coverlet it is."

"Ah, Your Majesty, but if you had the horse and the bell which belong to the dragon, you would then have nothing more to desire."

The King could not resist this possibility, so he issued another proclamation. As before, no one dared to answer, so Constantes was summoned to court again.

This time the King commanded, "You must return to the dragon's home to fetch me his special horse and bell. If you do not succeed, I shall kill you."

Now what was poor Constantes to do?

He left the King, pondering how he could obtain the horse and the bell. He knew that the horse would neigh, the bell would ring, and the dragon would waken to come down and eat him.

What could he do against the King's command? There was nothing for it but to set off as he had been ordered. Fortunately, he met the old woman again.

"Good day," he said, but sadly.

"The same to you, my son, and where are you going this time?"

"Don't ask," he said. "The King has ordered me to bring him the dragon's horse and bell, and if I don't he will kill me."

Again the old woman had a ready answer. "You must go back into town and ask for forty-one wooden plugs, for the bell has forty-one holes to be filled. Then you must hasten to the dragon's den. When you arrive, lose no time in plugging the holes in the bell—be sure you fill every one of them, for if you leave one unstopped, the bell will ring and the dragon will come out to eat you."

With care Constantes did all that the old woman told him to do, and he was able to get the bell and then the horse and to run away with them.

When the dragon woke up, he discovered that his bell and his favorite horse were both missing. Again guessing what had happened, he mounted another horse and caught up with Constantes close to the King's border.

"You villain," he cried. "Give back my horse and bell, and I will do you no harm."

But Constantes only replied, "What I have done so far is nothing. Just wait for what I shall do to you next."

The dragon rode hard, but Constantes rode hard too, so that the dragon could not catch him. Constantes was able to reach the King and present him with the horse and the bell. The King, in return, ordered two more suits, and Constantes went off about his business.

After another twenty days, the eldest brother once more went to the King and asked whether Constantes had brought him the horse and the bell.

The King answered that Constantes had done so, and very fine indeed were the dragon's horse and bell.

"Ah, Your Majesty! Now you've got these. But if you had the dragon himself to exhibit, then you could want nothing more."

This idea delighted the King. At once he issued a third proclamation: "Whoever is able to bring me the dragon so that I may show him in public, to him will I give a large kingdom."

Constantes's master soon brought word to him that he was to go and fetch the dragon.

But Constantes answered, "How can I fetch the dragon? He would make an end of me."

But his master said, "You cannot refuse to go."

So Constantes arose and went on his way. And as he tramped along he met the same old woman again, and greeted her with a "Good morrow, mother."

"Good day, my son. Whither away this time?"

"I am ordered to fetch the dragon for the King, and if I don't bring him, the King will kill me. Do tell me what to do, for this time I am sure I shall lose my life."

The old woman again had a ready answer. "You must not be dismayed, my lad. Go back and tell the King he must provide you with these things: a tattered suit, a hatchet and saw, an awl, ten nails, and four ropes. And when you have received these things and reached the dragon's property, you must put on the tattered garments and begin to hew down the tree which is outside the dragon's castle. When he hears the noise, he will come out and say, 'Good day to you! What are you laboring at, old man?' And you must answer, 'What do you think, my friend? I am working at a coffin for Constantes, who has died. I have been at work all this time and cannot cut the tree down.'"

Constantes repeated this while he got together the necessary tools and then proceeded to the tree outside the dragon's castle. He began to chop away, and he worked until the dragon heard the noise of the hatchet and came out of his castle.

"What are you doing here, old man?"

"I am working at a coffin for Constantes, who has just died," he replied. "But I cannot cut the tree down."

At this the dragon looked pleased. "Ah, the dog! Well, I shall soon manage it."

When the old man and the dragon together had made the coffin, the old man said to the dragon, "Get in and let us see if it is big enough, for you are the same size as he."

The dragon got into the coffin and lay down, whereupon Constantes picked up the coffin lid to see whether it fit. When he had laid it on, he quickly nailed it down and tied it tight. Then he lifted the coffin with the dragon in it onto his horse and rode away.

The dragon of course began to yell out, "Old man, let me out! The coffin fits!"

But Constantes answered, "Constantes has got you. He is taking you to the King, who wants to exhibit you in public!"

He carried the coffin to the King and said, "Now I have brought you the dragon to exhibit for the enjoyment of Your Majesty and all the people. But I ask that you fetch my eldest brother to open the coffin."

The King did as Constantes asked, and all the people gathered to look at the dragon.

When the eldest brother opened the coffin, the dragon, finding no one near him except the man who opened the lid, swallowed him in one gulp. This indeed was an exhibition—for all the crowd looking on from the casements and balconies of the palace. And it satisfied the King.

The Princess Who Loved Her Father Like Salt

O NCE UPON A TIME there was a King with three daughters. One day he sent for his daughters and asked each one how much she loved him.

The eldest said that she loved her father like honey. The second said that she loved him like sugar. And the third claimed that she loved him like salt.

When the King heard that from the young Princess, he was beside himself with anger. He went to the gate of the palace and stood there until he saw a poor man passing. To him he shouted that he would make him his son-in-law.

Amazed, the man replied, "My King, and many be your years, how shall I, a poor man, marry a Princess?"

"That is my wish," declared the King, and at once he handed over his daughter to be the fellow's wife.

What could the man do but accept the Princess, whom, of course, he admired very much. He took her home to his mother, who was very old, and they lived together as good friends, though in great poverty.

One day some rich merchants asked the poor man to accompany them on a distant journey. He agreed to go, for he thought this would help them all.

The party soon passed a well from which the man was ordered to fetch water. Scarcely had he begun to draw the water when a water spirit came up. The poor man was so astonished that he could only stammer, "G-good day, friend."

To this the water spirit replied, "Because of your kind greeting, I shall not devour you as I have others who came here to draw water. Instead, I give you these three pomegranates. But do not cut open these pieces of fruit until you are alone."

The poor man thanked the water spirit and hid the pomegranates in his pouch. He took the water to the merchants, and they all went on their way.

When the poor man met a traveler going the other way, he sent one of the pomegranates home to his wife and mother. As soon as this traveler had delivered it and gone on his way, the poor man's mother said to the Princess, "Let us cut it at once."

What magic! Instead of seeds, the pomegranate held diamonds, nothing but diamonds! These the women decided to sell so that they might build a proper house.

Since nothing was spared in the building, the house was so beautiful that it resembled a palace. To share their good fortune, the women provided a fountain for the pleasure of those who passed by.

Here in this fine establishment the Princess in time bore a son, and he grew into a fine boy in whom the two women took great joy. By the time the poor man returned to his village, the lad had become a tall, handsome youth.

When the poor man arrived at the place where his miserable hut had stood, he found the magnificent house. There he saw his wife sitting at the window with a fine-looking young man. He was puzzled, then filled with sudden anger. He was about to attack both his wife and the youth, for he thought the young man must have married his wife, but fortunately his wife recognized him. She turned to the young man and said, "Come, kiss your father's hand."

The poor man understood. He kissed both his wife and his son. But when he asked how she had managed to own such a house, she thought it a strange question. "Why," she said, "your own diamonds made it possible, those you sent us in the pomegranate."

Now all this long time the man had carried the other two pomegranates deep in his pouch, dried and forgotten. At once he searched for them, and when he found one and opened it, out poured diamonds to dazzle the eyes.

The lucky couple did not spend all this fortune on themselves. They gave freely to the poor and set up a shop where anyone could come and

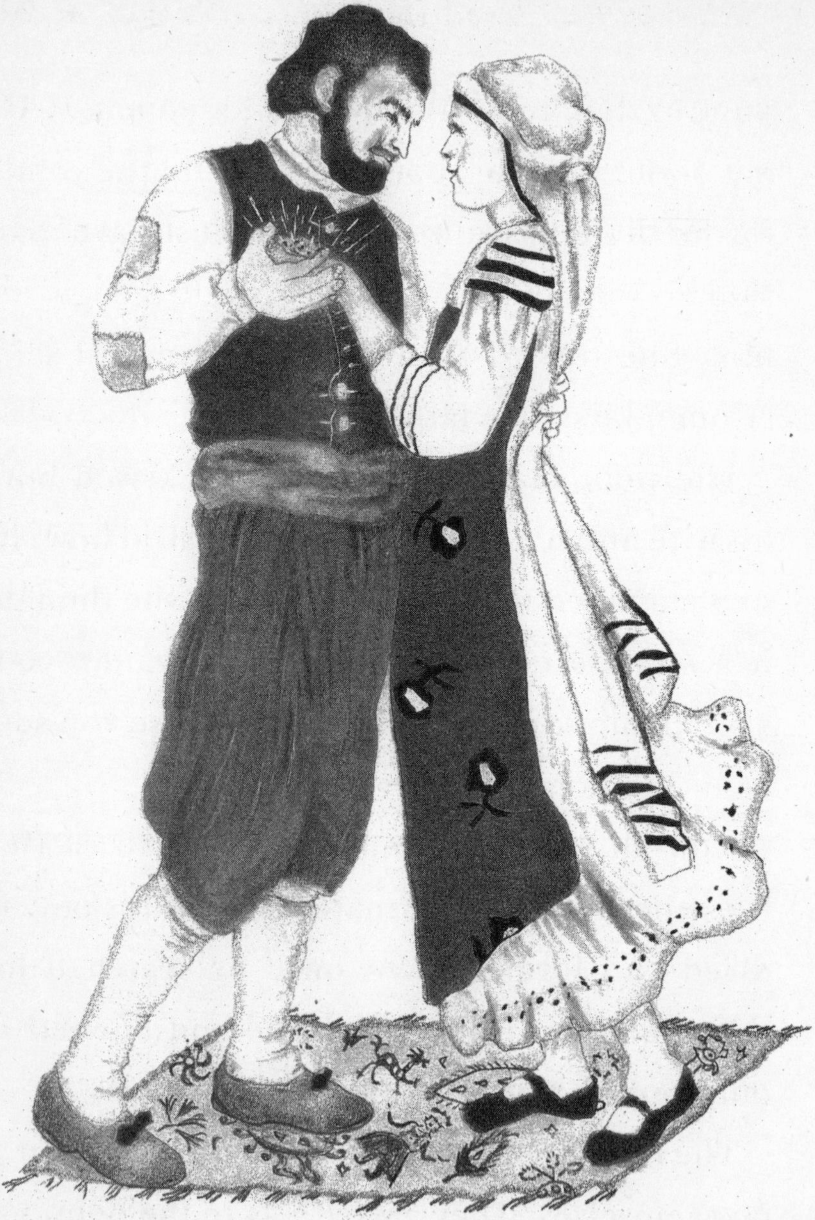

choose sweets without paying so much as the smallest coin. Such acts of charity came to the notice of the King himself. One day he asked his vizier, "Who is this man who gives such kindness to the poor? Let us see him for ourselves."

When the King and his vizier arrived, the Princess recognized her father, but she said nothing to him. To her husband, she remarked, "This evening we shall serve a special dinner to the King and his vizier." Thereupon she ordered the cook to prepare a number of dishes—half were to be cooked without salt, and half of them with salt.

That night, the first dishes to be served were those without salt. Neither the King nor his vizier could eat the tasteless food. These dishes were then removed, and the other food with salt was served. Now the men ate with relish.

When the King was asked how he liked the food, he replied, "The first had no salt and was uneatable. Food without salt is no good."

"Oh," said his daughter. "Do you remember, Father, that when I told you I loved you like salt, you drove me away?"

Surprised and ashamed, the King kissed his daughter and said, "Salt is better than honey and better than sugar."

The Foolish Wife and Her Three Foolish Daughters

ONCE UPON A TIME in Greece there was a priest who had a wife and three daughters. And I must tell you that all four women were an even match for each other in foolishness.

One day, after she had been to church, the priest's eldest daughter went for a walk outside the town. Seeing a steep cliff, she at once went to sit on the rim of it. But then she began to weep and wail. "Alas, to think that I shall one day marry and have a little child. He will come here and look over this cliff, and then he will fall over the edge and get killed. Alas, my darling, darling son!"

The other daughters were waiting at home for their sister, and at length one of them said, "Whatever can have become of our sister?"

The second one decided to look for her older sister, whom she found sitting on a rock, lamenting loudly.

"My dear sister," she cried, "what is the matter that you weep so loudly?"

"Alas!" replied her sister. "Don't you see this steep cliff? When I am married and get a little nephew for you, he will come here one day and tumble down and be killed!"

The second sister sat down, too, and she also began to cry. Lastly, the youngest sister came along searching for them and heard the same sad lament. And so, later, the mother also came and joined the weeping sisters, bewailing the sad fate of her grandson.

Now the good priest ran out to look for his family. As you well know, he found them sitting in a row, weeping and wailing more and more loudly. When he asked why they should be crying in this fashion, they answered that the eldest daughter was going to marry. She would have a little baby, and he would tumble down over the steep cliff and be killed!

The priest could only mutter, "Bless me! Bad luck take you all! How long am I to put up with your folly! Will you never learn sense! Heaven is my witness that I will get away from here, and leave you to your fate, or you will be the death of me!"

So he returned home, packed up, and departed, saying, "If I chance to find any three who are worse fools than you, and if fortune is kind and you live, I shall return and see you again. Otherwise, your eyes will lose their sight before you look on me once more."

With these plain words, the priest set out on his journey. He walked on until he came to another village. Here, passing a house, he heard loud wailing. When he peeped in to see what was going on, he beheld to his surprise a woman with a child in a cradle, and over the cradle a hatchet was hanging. It was the woman who was crying so loudly.

"Alas," she wailed. "My baby will be killed by a hatchet. My baby will be killed by a hatchet."

"My good woman," shouted the priest, entering the house, "whatever are you weeping about?"

"You ask me why I am weeping! Don't you see, your reverence, that this hatchet will fall and kill my child?"

"So, I'm not the only one," murmured the

priest to himself, and aloud he added, "What will you give me to save the baby from so sad a fate?"

"Whatever you please, your reverence. I would offer you my very life, if it were my own to give."

With that the priest moved the cradle to another part of the room. "There, there, good woman, now don't cry any more."

From the happy woman and her husband the good priest received a handsome gift, and then he started on with his travels.

Soon he came to another house, where a large crowd was gathered. More wailing and more loud shouts. The priest was naturally curious, so he drew close. At the door stood a tall man who was to go in and be married, but the door of his bride's house was so low that it appeared he could not enter. Everyone offered advice. He could cut off his feet, said one, and another advised that he could cut off his head. These

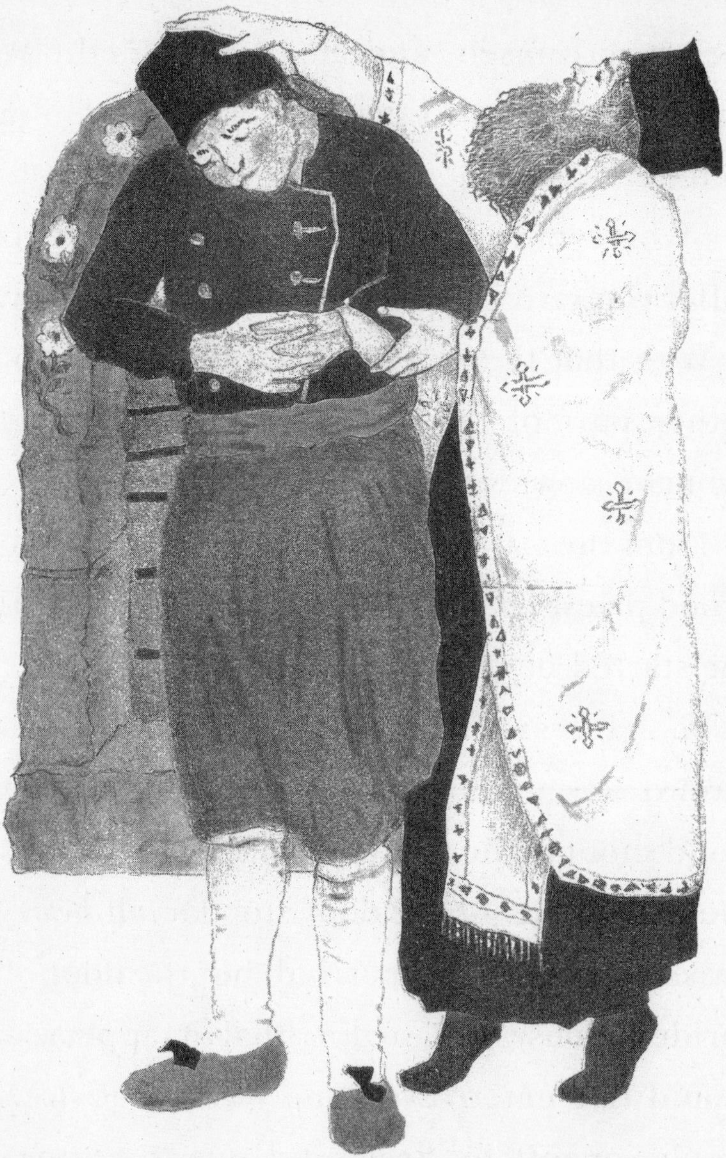

seemed the only possibilities. At this the priest began to shake with laughter.

"My fellows," he said—having some difficulty trying to hide his amusement—"what ails you that you stand here in a crowd shouting?"

When they told him the reason for their clamoring, the priest asked, "What will you give me if I get this good man into the house?"

"Take what you will. Only do us this favor!"

The priest thereupon took hold of the man's head. "Stoop a bit," he directed. "Now a little more, a little more," and he repeated this until the man was inside the door.

"There now," he said, "lift up your head again. And after this, as often as you go in and out, you must do the same. Do you understand?"

Since he was a priest, he then married the bride and groom and was off again on his way.

Only a bit farther on, he met an old woman washing a sow with great vigor. She proceeded to deck the animal with gold and silver spangles in preparation for a wedding. She begged the priest to lead the sow to the wedding, saying she was too old to travel. "I'll pay you well for the trouble," the woman said.

Such silliness the priest was willing to turn to his own advantage, so he agreed to regard it as a favor to drive the sow ahead of him. As soon as he had turned the corner, he stripped the sow of her gold and silver ornaments.

Thus laden, the priest returned to his wife. "I thought," said he, "that there could be none so foolish as you in all the world. But I have found that there are others who surpass you. I shall keep my word. Henceforth, I shall put up with you for better or for worse."

With the profits of his journey the priest provided handsome dowries for his daughters, and although his wife behaved foolishly from time to time, he lived happily with her forever after.

The Fairy Wife

D EMETROS the goatherd lived alone with his mother on the Keafa Hill. Near his hut and goat shed was a spring called the Fairy Spring, for the fairies had been seen there. Every day Demetros's mother carried her great earthen jar to this spring for water, but one day she fell ill, and Demetros went for water at night after he had driven his goats home.

In the moonlight he could clearly see three maidens in white sitting on stones around the

spring. Demetros paid them no attention until he had filled his jar, for he supposed them to be shepherdesses who had come for water. But when a cock's crow sounded across the valley, the maidens rose, joined hands, and danced westward across the hills. Singing and whirling faster and faster, they disappeared like a wisp of white smoke.

Demetros watched, full of wonder as to who they were, why they had come, and where they had gone. He said nothing about the strange maidens, but he thought of them all through the next day. And at night he went again to the spring. In the moonlight he saw six maidens this time, and once again as the cock crowed they rose, danced singing over the hills, and vanished.

Demetros filled his water jar and walked home, thinking. He was so quiet his mother asked if anything were wrong. He hesitated, then told her what he had seen on the two evenings.

"Beware, my son! The maidens may be fairies. Evil may come!"

For the third time Demetros went to the spring, and this time found nine maidens sitting on the stones. Once again the cock crowed and they danced away.

"Surely there can be no harm in watching them. They are so strange, so beautiful!"

This time Demetros forgot to fill his water jar and walked home with his eyes on the far hills where the fairies had disappeared.

"You must have seen the maidens again!" his mother cried, when she saw the empty jar. "To-morrow night brings the full moon when the fairies' power is greatest. Then you must not leave the goat shed."

Demetros intended to obey his mother, but all day as he watched his goats he thought of the maidens.

"I will not go tonight," he told himself. "I will

never see them again. I do not want to see them.
They might bring evil to my mother and me. I
will not see them—but how beautiful they were!"

That night he put his goats into the shed as
usual. Outside the door he looked up at the full
moon and remembered the last three nights.
How lightly the maidens had danced! How
brightly their golden hair had rippled over
their shoulders!

It was now almost midnight, and before
Demetros knew what he was doing, he found
himself hurrying toward the spring. He tried to
stop, but he could not. He reached the spring
and this time found ten maidens waiting for
him. He had found the nine maidens of the
night before lovely, but the tenth one they had
brought with them now was many times fairer.
She was more graceful, her hair was brighter,
and her face more beautiful than any maiden
Demetros had ever imagined.

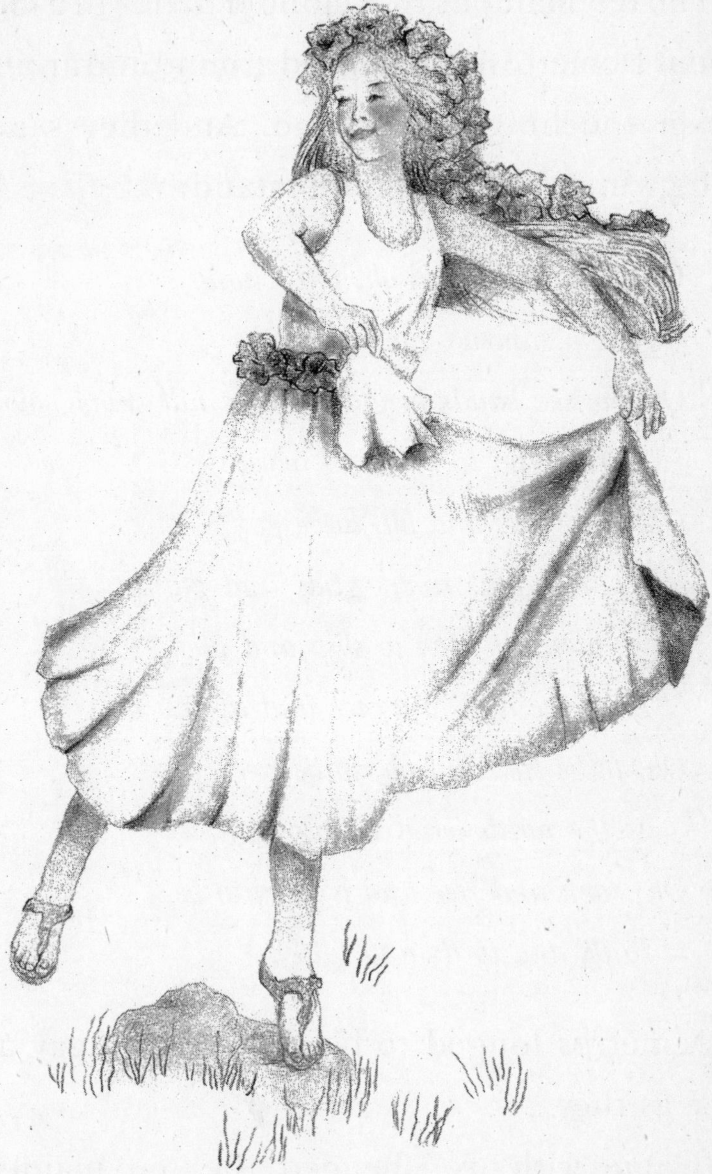

The ten maidens rose, joined hands in a circle about Demetros, and danced around and around, never touching the ground. And they sang a song which he could understand:

Oh, to be light and oh, to be light
  In the summer noonday sun;
On the sea sands bright and the hill snows white,
  To run and to run and to run!
Oh, to be gay and oh, to be gay
  Where bright rivers glide and glance;
In gardens of May to skip and play,
  To dance and to dance and to dance!
Oh, to be free and oh, to be free
  As the north wind riding high;
Oh, swift and free and a fairy to be,
  To fly and to fly and to fly!

Demetros longed to be as light and gay and free as they.

"Come with us," begged the ten maidens.

"Come with us, Demetros."

"Come and live in our palace with us," said the tenth fairy with her loveliest smile. "We shall make you happy, Demetros."

Unable to resist, he went with them a long way over the hills. He laughed and sang and forgot everything but the fairy maidens, their flowers, their smiles, their golden hair. Once he thought of his mother, ill and in need of him, and of his goats that would cry for him in the morning. He knew he should not go farther with the fairies, but when he looked at the tenth, the most beautiful one, he felt that he could not leave her as long as he lived.

Now she came near him in the dance. Her long golden hair swept past him. He breathed the fragrance of her flowers. He reached out to catch her, but caught only her handkerchief. At that moment the dance stopped and the fairies screamed. With a rush, like wind through a forest, they disappeared—all but the tenth. She sank down and hid her face in her hands.

For a long time Demetros stood looking down at this fairy maiden who had become his prisoner. He fell to his knees beside her and tried to comfort her, but nothing could stop her tears.

"Do not speak. Do not touch me," she said. "You have robbed me of my freedom, my happiness!"

Demetros stood up, tucked the handkerchief into his wide leather belt, and walked slowly away, full of wonder again. Looking back, he saw that she had risen and was following him, still weeping. He continued to walk, and she came, too, stopping when he stopped, moving forward as he did, until they had crossed the hills to his little hut.

Demetros's mother was startled to see this strange golden-haired maiden with her son. She welcomed her because she saw that Demetros loved her. She took the fairy handkerchief, wrapped it in silk, and locked it in her box away from the fairy wife.

Katena, as the beautiful fairy was called, spent her time now spinning, sewing, and embroidering. She made fine clothes for Demetros's mother, for herself, and for the little child that came to her and Demetros. Everyone in their village of Loutro knew that Katena was a fairy, because whatever she did was better work than anyone else could do in all their part of the country. The child, too, was very beautiful, with fine, golden hair. All the villagers and country people called her Neraidokoretso, which means fairy child.

But Katena was not happy, and nothing Demetros could do would make her smile. She never danced now or sang, but sat quietly at her work, scarcely speaking to anyone. Demetros grew sad, too, and to see him so unhappy made his mother grieve. This continued for seven years.

One St. Konstantinos Day, Demetros's mother went to a neighboring village to visit a cousin. She believed everything would be safe till her return.

But Katena said to Demetros, "Today is a holiday. I should like very much to go to Loutro to dance. I have not danced for a long time. Will you bring me one of my pretty dresses and my best handkerchief? We shall dance together as we danced under the full moon seven years ago."

Demetros could not speak for delight. His beautiful wife would dance and be happy again! He fumbled with the keys his mother had left in his care. He caught up the first dress his eyes fell upon. At length he found the beautiful hand-kerchief in his mother's box and with trembling hands folded it inside his belt. As soon as Katena was ready, she and Demetros with Neraidokoretso hastened down the hillside to Loutro.

In their bright costumes, joyous and graceful, the folk were already dancing on the grass plot in the center of the village. They formed a great circle, but instead of joining hands they faced each other in pairs holding a handkerchief stretched between each two of them. Katena and Demetros stepped into the circle, holding between them the fairy handkerchief which his mother had guarded these seven years.

Katena's turn came to lead the dance. Demetros dropped his corner of the handkerchief, and at once Katena sprang away, whirling madly about the circle. As Demetros watched her, amazed, she circled three times before the astonished villagers, then rose as though on wings and floated into the sky.

Demetros knew that his fairy wife had left him forever, and he wanted to die. His mother, returning from her cousin's, tried to console him. "My son," she said, "this is the evil which the fairy has brought upon us. Let us try to be content. Now nothing worse can come to us."

Demetros feared that his daughter would be unhappy without her mother, but every morning the child would hurry away to the fields and in the evening run home again, skipping and singing as she came. People said they often heard her talking or chanting to herself in words no one could understand.

Her grandmother was frightened at first because she could not induce the child to eat. One morning Demetros followed Neraidokoretso. He saw her go straight to the Fairy Spring and, looking up, hold her little arms toward the sky. He heard her calling and saw a white mist descend to her. A voice came out of the mist, and the child answered in words of a strange sound.

"It is Katena," he told his mother. "She must come every day to talk to Neraidokoretso and feed her fairy food. That is why she is in the fields all day and will eat nothing here. Katena is caring for her child."

As the years went by, Neraidokoretso grew more lovely, and more like her mother. When she went to the fields now she took her sewing or embroidery and worked while she talked with the spirit that no one else could see. Often Demetros followed her and watched. She was his daughter, but she never seemed to belong to him. She did not need him and was happy without him. It made him afraid, so that one day he said to his mother, "I believe something can happen to us worse than the trouble we have already suffered."

"How can that be, my son?" she asked.

"I am afraid that Neraidokoretso will not always be with us."

Demetros and his mother looked at each other without speaking. They both loved Neraidokoretso very much.

On the girl's fifteenth birthday Demetros followed her to the Fairy Spring, as he had done every day for so long a time. Again he saw the white mist come to her out of the clouds and heard the sweet voice. Today when she held up her arms, the mist enfolded her, lifted her up, and carried her away. After it had vanished, Demetros caught the echo of two fairy voices. He knew that Katena and Neraidokoretso had gone from him forever.

No longer did Demetros tend his goats. He wandered day after day through the fields and woods and over the hills, looking hopelessly for his wife and child. Sometimes a shepherd or goatherd, meeting him, would hear him chanting to himself:

Come back, come back, my fairy wife.
Come back, my fairy child.
Seeking and searching I spend my life;
I wander lone and wild.
Come back!

The Wonder
of Skoupa

ONCE UPON A TIME, on a stormy St. Nikolas Day, Vasilis the shepherd was keeping guard alone over silent fields in a valley below the snow-covered mountains. Christmas, or St. Nikolas Day as it is to the Greeks, is lonely on these peaks. Strange things can happen.

There was no company for Vasilis, for the other shepherds and goatherds with their flocks had sought shelter in the valleys. They would celebrate the festival with their friends and kinfolk in the villages.

At noon as Vasilis looked to the mountaintop above him, he saw what he thought was snow caught up in the wind and swirling around.

But then, from the spot where two mountain paths cross at the foot of a pine tree, he heard faint voices, like bells in the distance. Surely, he thought, no human being would have gone so far up on the mountain on St. Nikolas Day. Finally, Vasilis knew that the sweet voices and whirling whiteness were fairies dancing in a ring. He started forward to see them more closely, but at that instant they vanished and their voices died away.

Vasilis pressed on through the unbroken snow, but he could find no footprints nor anything else to reveal that fairies had visited the spot. Perhaps after all, it was not fairies he had heard, but only snow blowing in the wind. Then, almost hidden, he spied a bundle as white as the snow, and it stirred feebly.

Within the bundle Vasilis found a tiny baby, more beautiful than any child he had ever seen. Its fine hair shone golden as sunshine. Vasilis knew he had found a fairy child, and he marveled to think that he had indeed seen the fairies who had left it there.

In the village of Skoupa he stopped at each house to show the beautiful child and tell his story. The villagers were filled with awe. They decided together that they would care for the child in their own homes, turn and turn about.

And so it was done. They named the child Nikolas because he had been found on St. Nikolas Day. As he grew, he seemed to belong to

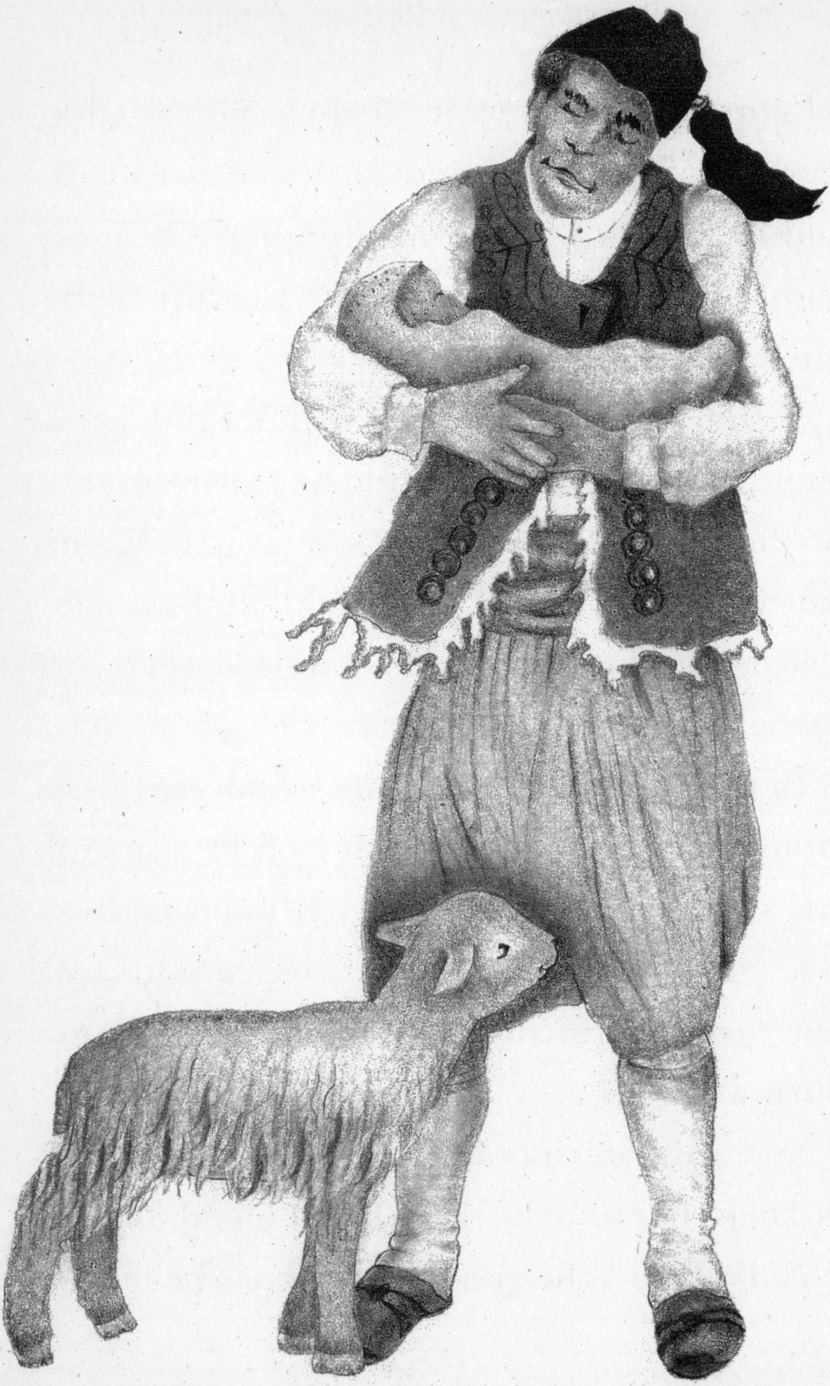

all the village folk, and he was loved by each. He received the same care as the other village children, the same food, and similar clothing. Yet from the beginning there was a difference. Not only was Nikolas handsomer than the rest and taller than any of his age, but he differed too in manner.

He was quiet. He did not play games with the others, but he would tell them wonderful stories, unlike any ever heard in Skoupa. Often he would wander away into the fields where some shepherd would come upon him gazing at the sky. Sometimes he did not seem to hear when he was spoken to. Because of his mysterious origin and his strangeness, he began to be known as the Wonder of Skoupa.

But at fifteen Nikolas became a shepherd and no longer needed the villagers' help. Like the other shepherds, he came down from the hills to spend a holiday in Skoupa, but he would not join in the games or dances. He would merely look on with sad and restless eyes. People wondered if he were thinking of his fairy mother and longing to go back to his kind. But because he was fairy-born, they dared not ask him.

Once again St. Nikolas Day came around— seventeen years after Vasilis had found the white bundle in the snow. Vasilis was now an aged shepherd, still guarding his flock on the silent hills. And every St. Nikolas Day he lived over in memory that strange day so long ago.

This year at noon he raised his eyes again to the pine tree at the crossroads high up on the mountain. This time, instead of a fairy ring of swirling white, he saw a man standing in the snow lifting his arms toward the sky. His head was bare and the sun fell on golden hair bright as the sunlight. Could it be anyone but Nikolas? Was he not spending the day in Skoupa?

Vasilis shaded his eyes against the sun's glare and gazed at the man, standing still there like a statue. The wind blew wisps of snow about him, and it grew thicker and thicker until the snow seemed to melt into the sky above the mountain peak. Suddenly Vasilis saw fairies, myriads of them all in white, dancing in the sky and in the whirl of snow about the motionless form. Faster and faster they danced until the cloud of them quite obscured the figure of the man. Their silvery voices, like the sound of distant bells, floated down to Vasilis. A sudden, fierce blast wrapped the mountaintop in a mist of flying snow and then just as suddenly passed, and the fairies and the man were seen no more.

Vasilis climbed to the crossroads and the tree. This time the fairies had left nothing behind. There was only trackless snow and the lonely pine tree.

Hoping against hope that it had not been Nikolas who had vanished from the mountain top, Vasilis plodded down to Skoupa to look for him. All the villagers joined him in his search, but none saw Nikolas that day, or any day again.

Fairy Gardens

UNCLE KOSTAS, as everyone called him, had once been a prisoner of the fairies. Now he would sit stiffly down upon a stone and lean on his tall shepherd's staff to tell his story.

"Look," he would begin, "do you see those hills yonder? They are the Hills of the Dragons." And he would recount what happened to him there many years ago.

Kostas the shepherd was napping at noon beside a spring, after eating his bread and cheese. When he opened his eyes, he saw fairies dancing around him. Some were singing, others playing their flutes. Now and then they begged him to play his flute with them. But when they saw his gun, their music and dancing suddenly ceased, and the fairies disappeared like a cobweb brushed away.

It was time for Kostas to go back to his sheep grazing below him on the hillside. But he found he could not move, not even his hand.

All at once the fairies were back and their Queen with them, riding on a great white horse. More and more fairies came, each on a white horse, until they covered Dragon Hill.

Kostas tried to stand up, to reach his gun, but he could only gaze at the beautiful Queen upon her proud horse, her silken hair shining and

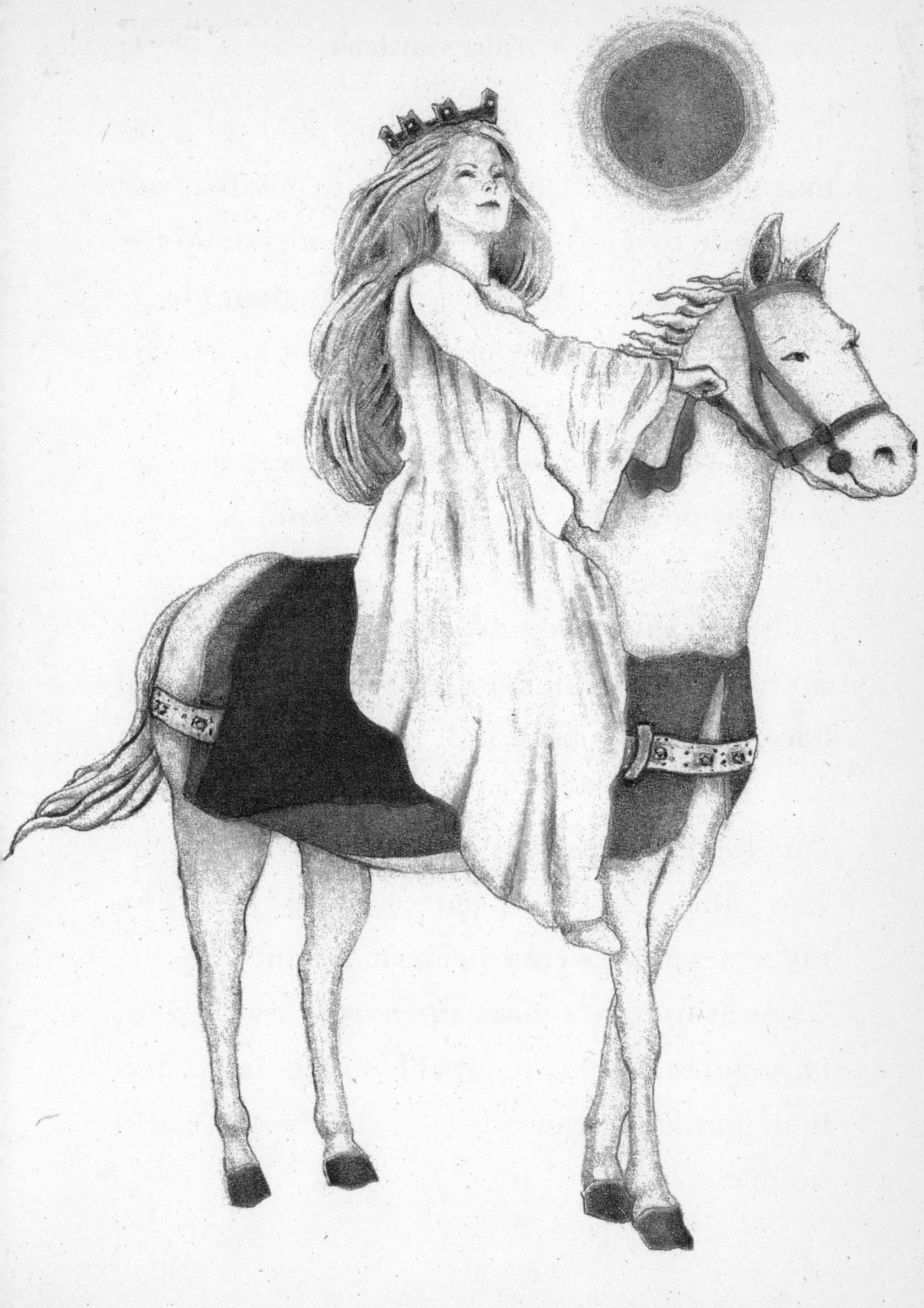

her white garments shimmering. A great murmuring filled the air, and to his surprise Kostas discovered that he could understand the fairies' speech. They were talking about him.

"Does he please you?" one fairy asked the Queen.

"Will you have him?" asked another.

"He is powerless now," said a third. "Shall we take him with us?"

The Queen looked down at Kostas for a long time. But then she smiled and cried, "I shall have him! He is beautiful! Let us take him with us!"

A cloud of fairies caught up Kostas and carried him with the speed of an eagle to the highest snow-covered peak of Mount Kyllene. There, through a black opening, down a dark passage, they came to a golden gate. It led into their gardens, where it is always sweet, warm summer.

Here you must stay
For a year and a day.
And never, oh never,
Will you wish to go away,

sang the Queen to her new prisoner, and all the fairies echoed:

And never, oh never,
Will you wish to go away.

Looking about, Kostas saw a true paradise. In a series of gardens grew flowers of different colors—white, yellow, purple, then green, rose, and blue, so that they blended into a rainbow.

On a lake of clear water an island appeared to float. Here played a band of youths, all stolen by the fairies. Kostas was brought to them, robed like them, and shown trees from which he might gather fruit. He found as many kinds of fruit trees as he had seen flower gardens around the lake. Figs, pears, olives, peaches, and plums, as well as grapes heavy upon their vines, hung there to tempt him.

Peacocks strutted about, and other birds of bright plumage flew among the trees. Mermaids, swans, and fish that were rare and unusual swam in the lake.

The Queen appeared happy, watching the fairies dance and make music and the youths playing their games.

Kostas alone was not happy. He could enjoy the riches, but he could not forget his home and his sweetheart, Christena. He longed for them, though he could believe that the Queen cared for him, more, perhaps, than for any of the other youths. He remembered her song:

> *Here you must stay*
> *For a year and a day,*
> *And never, oh never,*
> *Will you wish to go away.*

"I must wait," he told himself again and again. "I must wait for a year and a day."

At last the time had passed. Kostas could go to the Queen. Before her he bowed humbly, and said:

Here did I stay
For a year and a day,
But always and always
I've wished to go away.

He confessed to the Queen that although she was beautiful and her gardens were a true paradise, he desired above all else to go home to his sweetheart, Christena.

For a long time the Queen did not answer, and Kostas waited in anguish.

"Kostas," she said at last, "will you do anything I ask?"

"Anything!" he cried, starting up eagerly.

"Listen, then. By noon today, you must find

my lost treasure. It is a gold vase set with turquoise and it is lined with golden hair. Be sure of the lining of golden hair, for that is important. Go, then, and find it!"

Kostas began his search in the gardens, but though he looked carefully, among all the many flower beds, he found nothing. He searched beneath all the fruit trees on the island, and he scanned their branches. But there was no vase.

Now it was almost noonday. He stood looking hopelessly into the clear water of the lake when suddenly he spied a strange fish, all gold and blue. It was swimming toward him. But no, it was not a fish. It was a vase, and it was gold set with turquoise!

Kostas seized it and held it up. The lining! He was almost afraid to look, but there it was, the fine gold hair. And inside there was something else—more precious to him than hair or jewels or gold. It was his shepherd's clothing, which he had worn on the day the fairies carried him away. Now he knew that the Queen meant to let him go.

Quickly exchanging the fairy garments for his old loose cloak and short, full shepherd's skirt, he returned to the Queen and laid her vase before her.

The Queen smiled and said, "You may go now to your home and your sweetheart. And you may take with you a strand of the hair from the vase. It is my hair, and if you should ever wish to return to the gardens, you have only to show it to the fairies and they will bring you back."

Kostas thanked her many times and arose. He found a beautiful white horse ready to carry him away and three princesses to point the direction. Through the golden gate, down the long, dark passage to the snow-fringed opening in the mountain, and over the hills they flew—

until they reached the spring on the Dragon Hill. There the fairies left him, just where he had been a year and a day before. Kostas was free to go to his Christena.

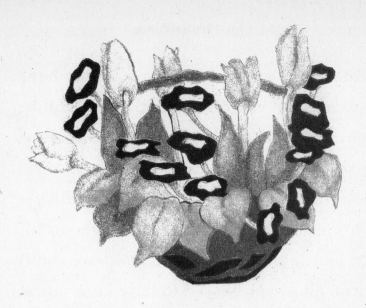

The First of May

ANASTO was the unhappiest of all the maidens in the village of Pyrgos, and it was all because she was the most beautiful. The other maidens were jealous of her. They would not sit with her or talk with her, and they were all too ready to gossip about her. Anasto lived in a little house a bit apart from the other village houses with her uncle, who was too old to work. They were very poor.

But Anasto was loved by Tassos, a shepherd who tended his sheep on the slopes of Helmos. Anasto knew he loved her, and the villagers of Pyrgos knew it. Tassos was handsome, and he sang better than any other man in the village. When his voice rang out, rich and beautiful, from up on the hills, any of the maidens would have given all she possessed to have known that his song had been for her. However, it was always to Anasto that he sang from his hillside above her home.

Tassos's love was the only joy Anasto knew, and even this was dimmed by the jealous girls. But old Malamo, who was called a sorceress, was kind to Anasto. She would say to the villagers: "You know that Anasto is beautiful, and on that account you are envious. Naught but evil can come to cruel persons who make unhappy an innocent child like Anasto!"

Many times Malamo repeated this, and each

time the girls would tell her to go back to her magic and her fairies and leave mortals to their own ways.

Now it was the custom on the first of May for the maidens to rise early, before dawn, and to go with their flower baskets to the stream at the foot of Mount Helmos to perform their May Day rites. This year they did not notice that Anasto was not with them, so great was their haste to be up on the hills before sunrise.

Each maiden held in her right hand a silver coin which she had saved for this occasion. Standing on the bank of the stream, the maidens threw the coins into the water so they could wash their hands and touch the fairies' flowers without harm. In unison they chanted:

O kindly stream, may I partake
Of all your cool delights,
And may I be forever free
From the power of your sprites.

The maidens then joined hands and danced among the rocks along the water's edge. As the light in the east grew brighter, they broke away from each other and climbed the winding paths up the hills in search of flowers for their hair and for their baskets.

Anasto was the last to come to the river, and she was alone. She stood there, looking into the bright water, but she had no coin to give to the stream. Hers was a sad voice that began the familiar chant:

O kindly stream, may I partake. . . .

She broke off, sobbing. Her empty flower basket rolled away as she fell to the ground. Without the coin, she could not touch the water and could not gather the fairy flowers. Bitterly she wept, and her tears fell into the stream. The waters darkened and the waves moaned, "Anasto, your tears have embittered us!"

The wild flowers also cried out, "Anasto, your tears have poisoned the water that we drink. Our petals are fading!"

And the birds joined in, "Anasto, your tears have embittered the seeds that we eat and the fruits of the trees, and our hearts are embittered!"

But Anasto could not listen. She continued to weep and her tears mingled with the river waters. The sun had climbed high and now stood above the stream. It was midday, the hour of fairies. Anasto's eyes were so dimmed by tears and her senses so dulled by weeping that she was not aware of the cloud of fairies suddenly surrounding her, nor did she hear their strange music and fairy voices.

"How beautiful she is!" exclaimed one of the fairies.

"She has cast no silver coin into the water," said the fairy Queen in anger.

"She is dropping her silver tears," said another fairy tenderly.

"Her tears have darkened our stream and the waters are saddened!" cried the Queen. "Seize her. She is in our power. Away with her to the peak of Helmos!"

But then the fairies noticed the charm that Anasto always wore for protection against evil. It had come down to her from an ancestor and hung around her neck on a silken thread.

"It is a magic stone," said the fairies.

"Touch it not," commanded the Queen. "Come! We must leave this maiden here."

The fairies abandoned Anasto in a rocky cave where no mortal had ever ventured to set foot.

When it was sunset, the maidens of Pyrgos came singing and dancing down from the slopes of Helmos, their heads crowned with wreaths of blossoms and their baskets full of flowers and green branches. As each one reached her own home, she hung flower garlands on the door and fastened the branches above it, so that the whole village had its May Day look of a garden bower.

From his hillside Tassos watched for Anasto to return with the maidens. When he saw that she was not among them, he ran down to the village. He found all the doors except Anasto's hung with the May Day garlands. When he questioned the maidens, they could tell him nothing. Tassos found no trace of her except her little empty flower basket at the edge of the river.

Again and again Tassos shouted out Anasto's name, but only the echo of his voice rang back to him from the rocks above. Up into the hills he ran, still crying, "Anasto, Anasto!" and he did not cease, though it had grown dark. All night he searched among the pines and firs and rocks, without success.

At dawn Tassos came again to the stream, calling, "Anasto, Anasto!" Looking into it, he groaned, "O cruel stream, where is my Anasto?" His tears, too, fell into the silvery waters, turning them dark as the waters moaned. Tassos looked toward Pyrgos and cried out against the village that had made Anasto unhappy.

Even as he spoke, dark clouds began to mass above the village. In a moment the heavens were covered and the brightness of dawn was blotted out. Lightning and thunder followed, and hail fell upon the land.

"Let Pyrgos be destroyed!" cried Tassos, leaping up in a fury of grief and anger. "Let it be wiped out! It has persecuted my Anasto!"

The old sorceress, Malamo, saw the doom of the village in the dark sky. Running out, she called to the villagers, "The punishment for your cruelty is at hand. Your homes and all of you will be destroyed. Come, follow me, if you would save your village! Follow me to the stream, if you would not die! Bring a stone. We will stone the stream. We will stone the stream!"

Terror filled every heart. All the people of Pyrgos followed Malamo to the riverbanks. When she cast her stone into the stream, the others did the same. They pressed about her. "Tell us what to do," they begged.

"The fairies of the stream have taken away your Anasto," explained the sorceress, "and you have avenged yourselves upon them. The stream is stoned. Now let all the maidens search in the caves of Helmos, for in one of them Anasto is hidden. Let them not return without her, for if they do, great will be the evil upon this village!"

Tassos, who had watched this scene, led the maidens, lighting their way by torches, up to the dark caves of Helmos.

All that dark day they searched, until at last on the mountain peak where none before had dared to venture, they came upon Anasto in the fairy cave, alone. She could not move, nor could she speak, or show by any sign that she saw them. The maidens wept in despair, but Tassos took Anasto in his arms. When he brought her out upon the mountainside, the sky cleared at once. The last rays of daylight fell upon them, and Anasto opened her eyes. She looked about, she smiled, and she called each of them by name.

A rejoicing procession brought the lost maiden down from the hills. A wreath was put upon her head; her basket was filled with flowers; the other maidens held her hands. And for three days the village held a festival with music, flowers, and dancing to celebrate her return. Happiest of all were Anasto and her devoted Tassos.

Fairy Mother

ONCE UPON A TIME on the island of
Crete there was a youth called Kapetanakis, whose father had been a
Kapetan or leader. The father's death had made
the boy an orphan. Kapetanakis was a handsome boy, and he pleased everyone with the
sweet sounds he called from the strings of his
lyre.

From his early boyhood Kapetanakis liked to climb to the highest peak on his island. There he would sit for hours playing his lyre, gazing down at the blue sea that gives Crete its name, the Blue Island. Sometimes the village maidens would leave their work to listen to his music as it sounded down over the land. The villagers could imagine him to be an eagle, sitting so high up there on the mountain.

But Kapetanakis was lonely. Often he gazed far out to sea as though he heard, above the sound of his own playing, someone calling him from the silent waters.

One noon in autumn while he was lying half asleep in the dark shadows of the fir trees near the Spring of Dreams, he suddenly sat up. He had heard singing, and with it the music of flutes and the throbbing of a drum up in the hills. "Perhaps," he thought, "someone is coming to me and I shall not be lonely anymore."

As the sounds grew louder, there appeared three strange maidens, wearing long veils sparkling with gems and golden sandals adorned with jewels.

The maidens came nearer, two playing flutes and the third singing and gently beating a drum. They danced around the spring without appearing to see Kapetanakis, then they flitted from hill to hill, from spring to spring, and finally skimmed across the sea to vanish on the horizon. They left with Kapetanakis only the echo of their music and the memory of their bright garments.

At the same hour next day, Kapetanakis took his place again at the spring and played on his three-stringed lyre, trying to create the silver, bell-like beauty of the maidens' melodies. Then again, sounds of unearthly sweetness floated up to him and he saw the three strange maidens dancing toward him. He held his breath. His lyre fell from his hands. The maidens danced nearer and nearer till he could breathe the perfume of their garments and feel the air stirred by their dancing steps. Wild with joy, he leaped up to dance with them, only to see them flit lightly away, circle about the mountain peak and pass beyond, growing smaller and smaller till they disappeared where the sky and sea meet.

"What are they?" he asked of the spring. "Why do they come?" he asked of the fir trees. "They do not even see me! Oh, if they would stay, if they would speak to me!" He looked about at the rocks and hills and sky, but there was only silence everywhere.

On the third day at noon, Kapetanakis waited again at the spring. At last, faintly came the music of the flutes, then the glint of the gems, and the swirl of airy garments.

Kapetanakis stood up as the veiled maidens drew near. He held his hands out toward them. He cried to them to stop, but they did not notice him, and his voice was drowned in their music. Once more they circled about him, and started away.

But Kapetanakis could not let them go. Madly he plunged after them and seized the veil of the one nearest. She shrieked. The two others darted with the speed of a kite straight out to sea and vanished, while the third, her face unveiled, gazed after them in terror and dismay.

To Kapetanakis the beauty of the maiden before him rivaled that of the goddess Aphrodite. What was she? He wanted to ask, but he was afraid. At the end of a long moment she turned slowly toward him, with a look of such sadness that he dropped to his knees.

"Oh, do not be sad," he begged. "Only stay with me, and I shall make you happy!"

The maiden was silent.

"Please speak!" he pleaded. "Speak to me and tell me that you will stay and be happy!"

At length the maiden looked at him and asked, "Why did you do this?"

Kapetanakis had never heard such a beautiful voice.

"Speak again!" he cried. "I love you. I want you for my wife." And he called her Agnoste, meaning Unknown One.

Agnoste, after a long silence, said, "I shall marry you on one condition."

"Only one!" he exclaimed. "What is it?"

"I am a fairy, whom you have in your power. The condition is that I shall never speak again."

"I would accept any condition," answered Kapetanakis, although he was disappointed.

So they were married. They built a little home

at the foot of a mountain, and after three years an elflike child was born to them.

Kapetanakis had hoped that his love for Agnoste would break her vow of silence, but she only followed him wordlessly. Even to their child, Agnoste never spoke. But this fairy child, with her strange, quiet ways, seemed not to be unhappy because of her mother's silence.

One day Kapetanakis said to himself that this could not last. He must find some way to make Agnoste break her silence.

That evening with great fervor Kapetanakis sang a song of entreaty to Agnoste, but his words were useless.

The next morning Kapetanakis left the house early to climb the mountain path. Agnoste followed with their child in her arms.

On top of the hill Kapetanakis set to work on a plan. He gathered branches and leaves for a fire. Not knowing his intention, Agnoste laid

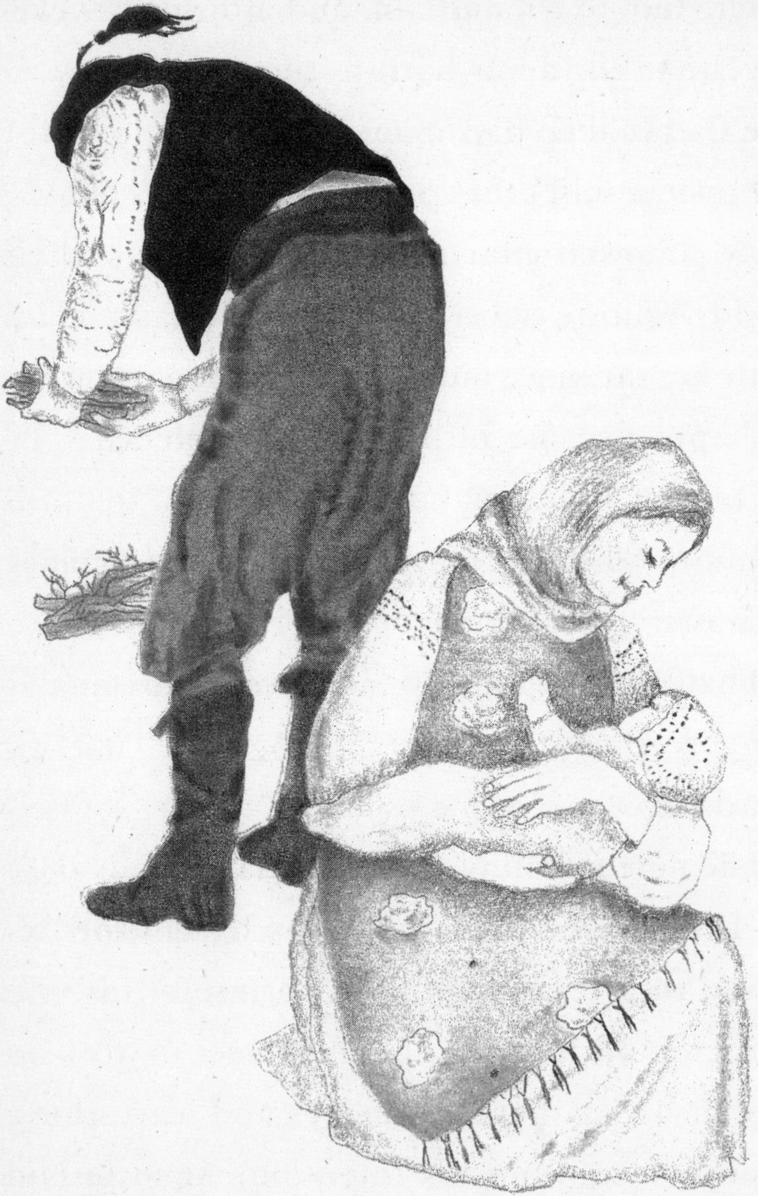

their child down and helped him. Kapetanakis set fire to the heap, and together they watched the flames leap high toward the sky.

Kapetanakis then picked up their sleeping child. "Surely," he thought, "Agnoste must speak when she imagines I am about to cast our child into the flames!" He approached the pile, lifted the child high, and swung his arms as though he would hurl her into the fire.

But Agnoste leaped into the air, grasped the child, darted straight through the flames, and without a sound flew over the hills and was lost on the gray-blue horizon of the sea. Strange sounds came from the fire which, like a snuffed candle, died out the instant Kapetanakis turned to it. For hours he stood motionless before its ashes, then set out on a wild search for his wife and child.

No longer was Kapetanakis to be seen sitting eagle-like on the mountain, nor his lyre to be heard among the hills. He climbed the mountain peaks, he wandered through woods and fields seeking the palace of the fairies.

After many years the people of the island one day again saw Kapetanakis high on the mountain. The notes of his lyre sounded sweet as in the old days, though sad. But when the villagers reached the rock on which he had been sitting, he was gone, and they did not see him again.

About This Series

I N RECENT DECADES, folk tales and fairy tales from all corners of the earth have been made available in a variety of handsome collections and in lavishly illustrated picture books. But in the 1950s, such a rich selection was not yet available. The classic fairy and folk tales were most often found in cumbersome books with small print and few illustrations. Helen Jones, then children's book editor at Little, Brown and Company, accepted a proposal from a Boston librarian for an ambitious series with a simple goal — to put an international selection of stories into the hands of children. The tales would be published in slim volumes, with wide margins and ample leading, and illustrated by a cast of contemporary artists. The result was a unique series of books intended for children to read by themselves — the Favorite Fairy Tales series. Available only in hardcover for many years, the books have now been reissued in paperbacks that feature new illustrations and covers.

The series embraces the stories of sixteen different

countries: France, England, Germany, India, Ireland, Sweden, Poland, Russia, Spain, Czechoslovakia, Scotland, Denmark, Japan, Greece, Italy, and Norway. Some of these stories may seem violent or fantastical to our modern sensibilities, yet they often reflect the deepest yearnings and imaginings of the human mind and heart.

Virginia Haviland traveled abroad frequently and was able to draw upon librarians, storytellers, and writers in countries as far away as Japan to help make her selections. But she was also an avid researcher with a keen interest in rare books, and most of the stories she included in the series were found through a diligent search of old collections. Ms. Haviland was associated with the Boston Public Library for nearly thirty years— as a children's and branch librarian and eventually as Readers Advisor to Children. She reviewed for *The Horn Book Magazine* for almost thirty years and in 1963 was named Head of the Children's Book Section of the Library of Congress. Ms. Haviland remained with the Library of Congress for nearly twenty years and wrote and lectured about children's literature throughout her career. She died in 1988.